The Ice Cream Crown Skating Races

AMY LAURENS

OTHER WORKS

SANCTUARY SERIES
Where Shadows Rise
Through Roads Between
When Worlds Collide

KADITEOS SERIES
How Not To Acquire A Castle

STORM FOXES SERIES
A Fox Of Storms And Starlight
A Stag Of Snow And Memory

SHORTER WORKS
All The Thing We Saved You From
Bones Of The Sea
Christmas Miracle Is Just A Saying
Dreaming of Forests
Rush Job
Trust Issues

COLLECTIONS
And Then I Shall Transform
April Showers
Darkness And Good
It All Changes Now
Of Sea Foam And Blood
The Inklet Collection

POETRY & PLAYS
Change Becomes Us
For A Little While
Where Your Treasure Is

NON-FICTION
How To Write Dogs
How To Theme
How To Create Cultures
How To Create Life
How To Map
How To Plan A Pinterest-Worthy Party Without Dying
On The Origin Of Paranormal Species
The 32 Worst Mistakes People Make About Dogs

Find other works by the author:
www.AmyLaurens.com

The Ice Cream Crown Skating Races

AMY LAURENS

AUSTRALIA

Paperback ISBN: 978-1-922434-96-8
Hardcover ISBN: 978-1-922434-75-3
eBook ISBN: 9798227197504

www.inkprintpress.com

National Library of Australia Cataloguing-in-Publication Data
Laurens, Amy 1985 –
The Ice Cream Crown Skating Races
106 p. cm.
ISBN: 978-1-922434-96-8
Inkprint Press, Canberra, Australia
1. Juvenile Fiction—Fantasy & Magic 2. Juvenile Fiction—Mysteries & Detective Stories 3. Juvenile Fiction—Sports & Recreation—Ice Skating 4. Juvenile Fiction—Family—Siblings

Summary: George must win the Ice Cream Crown Races, skating on magically deep-frozen ice cream, if he wants his family to keep their home.

Third Edition: June 2024

This book was written on Ngunnawal country, and the author and publisher would like to acknowledge the people who have told their stories here for countless generations.

For the Canberra Write Like An Author crew of July 2021. Thanks for the inspiration. You guys are fabulous <3

CHAPTER 1

THE ICE CREAM CROWN SKATING RACES DREW SOMETHING like half a million people to the little town of Linderch every year, and even though it was only ten a.m. on the first day of practices, George thought that at least half of those people must already be here.

That was what it felt like, anyway, pushing and elbowing his way through a crowd of mostly adults, mostly a head taller than him, trying not to drop his hotdog as he squished and squeezed his way back toward the sheep-panel fence that blocked the skating pond from the spectators.

Deep fried snacks scented the air, smells that seemed warm even in the middle of a snowy winter, with air that pinched at George's nose and slapped at his cheeks.

He bit into the hotdog, trying to scoff it down before it either went cold or got knocked out of his hands in the press of people. Someone elbowed him in the back and he stumbled, juggling the rest of the hotdog awkwardly in his red gloves... But he caught it in time and the crowd opened up enough of a gap for him to dart a bit closer to the fence.

He shrugged his shoulders, nestling his mustard-coloured puffer jacket up around his ears.

Around him, the crowd muttered and chattered and murmured—and someone was shouting. George stood on tiptoes to see—the voice sounded familiar.

Ah, it was old Avi, arguing with a race official over by the competitor's gate. George stared in fascination. This was the third argument George had seen Avi having today, and the grounds had only been open for two hours. Not that that was unusual for Avi, a dark skinned, white-haired, gnarled old fellow who seemed to have a bone to pick with every person whose shadow crossed his path.

The first argument George had witnessed today had been with one of the ice cream stalls about the size of the scoops they were handing out (too irregular, some big, some small). The second had been with a fluffed-up snow goose over Avi's ice cream cone (the goose had won, stealing the cone right out of Avi's hand). And now, he was ranting about something to do with potholes.

George rolled his eyes. He jostled his way to the railings that held the crowd back from the pond and leaned his elbows on it. Around him, the crowd shuffled and muttered and murmured, boots slushing in the half-melted snow, voices rising and falling like the wind.

George let it all wash over him, eyes on the pond, searching out Mabel.

It was hard to spot her pastel pink coat against the swirling, pastel rainbow of the surface on which the competitors skated; ribbons of mint green and banana yellow and bubblegum pink twined through the frozen pond, cut through with slashes of baby blue and lavender.

The pond looked good enough to eat—and that was almost entirely the point.

Sponsored by the Linderch Ice Cream Museum, the Ice Cream Crown Skating Races took place not on ice, but on magically deep-frozen ice cream—an entire pond full of it. No one quite knew how the Museum convinced the ice cream to set solid enough to skate on—let alone how they procured *enough* ice cream to keep the pond filled throughout the winter—but regardless, it was *the* event of the Linderch calendar, drawing tourists from far and wide and filling the whole town with delicious, sugary smells for a month every year.

And then, of course, there were the promotional stands set up at regular intervals the whole way around the pond. Also sponsored by the Ice Cream Museum, for one hour every day in the month-long lead up to the races, you could brave the crowds and the queues and take your shot at some free ice cream—assuming the line moved fast enough that you got to the front of it before the hour was up.

George had finished his triple-caramel twist in a choc-dipped waffle cone just minutes before, and the delicious, sugary taste still lingered.

A red streak caught George's eye. Landon, Mabel's primary competition. George frowned. Landon's form was on point, his spins sharp, and his slaloms... George winced as Landon zipped precariously close by someone in a pink jacket.

But Mabel, in her pink jacket, continued unfazed by Landon's theatrics, and George smiled. Sure, the competition was stiff and the family was in danger of losing the house, but anyone who thought Mabel wasn't a shoe-in to win clearly hadn't seen her practice. She kicked out right atop a mint-green spiral, leapt, spun... and spun... and slipped.

George's gasp echoed through the crowd as the spectators watched Mabel fall. As the favourite in the Junior Division, her face had been plastered all over town for the last few weeks; everyone knew who she was, and George had to imagine that quite a few of them would be genuinely sad to see a favourite stumble like that.

The gasps swelled to muttering, and then to outright ripples of concern and worry as Mabel struggled to regain her footing. She managed to drag herself upright—but only just. George squinted; her right leg wasn't working properly.

His stomach twisted, hot adrenalin bursting through him as he watched her struggle the thirty yards to the shore and realised that, in one, short fall, Mabel had just plummeted out of the favourites.

The muttering around him was definitely concern, but not all of it was for Mabel; a fair proportion was worry for the mutterers themselves, people who'd placed bets on Mabel to win, or at least to place highly in the races.

George let out a tight breath, the air misting in front of his face, and gripped the rail tightly. "*Come* on, Mabes," he whispered. "You'll be alright." He shouldered his way to the right, closer to the gate where the contestants could exit the skating area, all the while keeping his eyes on that pastel pink coat.

"Nasty fall there."

The acid tone of voice snagged George's attention, paired with an uncomfortable shiver. His eyes narrowed at the sight of Max (first name? last name? nobody knew) from the bank, his light brown hair standing out amidst the colourful crowd of knitted beanies, hoods and headscarves.

George couldn't help himself. "Why should you care?" he said scathingly. "I'd have thought you'd be *glad*." If anyone was going to be glad that Mabel couldn't compete—couldn't *win*, which included the fairly large cash prize—it was Max, who'd been angling to have the bank take George and Mabel's family house as long as they could remember.

Max smiled unpleasantly. "Why would I be glad that someone had gotten injured? That would be rather... childish."

George opened his mouth.

"George!"

He glanced around; Josef, one of the security guards patrolling the entrance to the skaters-only area, waved at George over the heads of the crowd, motioning him toward the gate.

George turned back to cut Max one last glare, but he'd gone, shifting on with the natural eddies of the crowd.

A hurried scuffle later and George made it to the gate, and Josef was ushering him through. "Go help her," he said, shooing George into the skaters-only area.

George took a brief moment to throw Josef a word of thanks—and to thank his lucky stars that it had been Josef on duty today, who not only knew that Mabel and George were siblings, but suspected more than anyone else what this contest meant to them.

Then he was slipping and skidding and sliding down the slight incline that led to the shore of the ice cream pond, and Mabel was collapsing against him, and he was clutching at her upper arms to hold her up.

"It's my ankle," she gasped out, eyes wide, brows tight with pain. "I think it's broken."

George shook his head. "You should have called a medic." Trust Mabel to insist on skating all the way back to shore on a broken bone.

Of course, maybe it was only a sprain... but Mabel's pain threshold was famously high, so really, all George could do was shake his head again and pull her tight against him.

"Come on," he said, turning and hefting her onto his back so he could trudge through the slurry of the landing zone toward the medic's tent, cardinal red and so bright against the snow it might as well have been blood.

The medic met them at the door of the tent, a frown twisting his face behind his fluoro-green glasses. A label on his navy shirtfront read 'Lucas / Medic', with the ice cream castle logo of the Ice Cream Museum on the left.

"Which leg?" he said, his tone brusque and no-nonsense.

"My right," Mabel said.

Those who didn't know her might have been surprised at the levelness of her voice—but George's stomach twisted again unpleasantly. Usually, Mabel's voice was full of emotion and drama—sometimes good, sometimes bad. She only sounded calm like this when something was seriously wrong.

As they entered the tent, the scent of eucalyptus disinfectant clouded around them. George let Lucas The Medic slide Mabel off his back, then helped as she hobbled to the portable hospital cot. Gingerly, Mabel perched on the white sheets while Lucas The Medic knelt on the thick grey marine carpeting that covered the ground and began removing her skates.

The light from the overhead lamps flooded the room, washing out colours and glinting off the sharp blades of the skates as Lucas set them aside.

George stared, numb, looking through the scene rather than at it as Lucas manipulated Mabel's ankle back and forth.

Once, he glanced at Mabel's face; even allowing for the way the fluorescent lighting leached away all colour, her face was pale, drawn.

He shivered.

"I'm sorry," Mabel said in a tiny voice, and George realised she'd seen him shiver as he looked away. "I'm so sorry."

Abruptly, as though the strings holding him up had been cut, George slumped onto the cot beside her. It creaked as he added his weight. "It's not your fault. Hey, it's not," he added, bumping her gently with his shoulder as she inhaled sharply, the sound a precursor to a sob.

"I know," she moaned. "But the *house*."

George closed his eyes and let her lean against him. The house, the house. It all came back to the house, didn't it.

Their family lived in a sandstone house that was old, and kind of falling down. Partly, that was because George and Mabel's mum and dad had fallen on hard times recently and didn't have the money for repairs. But partly, it was because the house was special.

In the sitting room at the front, the walls were mustard yellow and the carpet navy blue. It smelled of baked cabbage on Tuesdays, and on Thursdays odd-looking rainbows refracted over the ceiling despite the absence of anything to cause them.

The kitchen seemed normal enough, if somewhat small and pokey… But if you walked in sideways, with your left arm leading the way, the view out the window shimmered into something otherworldly, and once or twice George was positive he'd seen a unicorn saunter past.

The bathroom tasted like bubble gum constantly; the dining room floor creaked to the tune of 'Happy Birthday' if you hopped only on your right foot; and George's own bedroom occasionally lit up with aquamarine ripples like light shining through water, accompanied by the smell and taste of the sea.

George's sister Mabel had sworn the other day she'd even heard a seagull when she'd been passing by his door (and not at all sneaking into his room to borrow his set of expensive, brightly coloured markers).

It was a wonderful house, magical, and if the family couldn't find the money to pay back the overdue part of the mortgage in the next five weeks, they would lose it.

How could you move back into a regular, normal house after living in one filled with magic? George and Mabel didn't think they could bear it.

So they'd come up with a plan.

George and Mabel hadn't told their parents that they were planning for Mabel's winning from the Ice Cream Crown Skating Races to pay for the house...

...And now, it seemed like even that last, desperate option was gone.

George sighed, eucalyptus filling his nose again as he concentrated on his breaths. "You're not going to be able to compete, are you?"

Mabel turned her big eyes on him. "I'm so sorry," she whispered, and she looked like she was in more pain now than she had when Lucas was manipulating her ankle.

George shook his head firmly. "I'll do it," he said.

Mabel blinked. "What?"

"I'll do it. I know I don't have much time to get back up to speed, but we've got to try, we just have to. It's our last hope."

Mabel's smile was midway between hope and despair, but regardless it was a smile and George was going to take that and be glad for it. "I'll help you," she said.

"I know."

He probably wouldn't win, but he had to try. He had to. Their wonderful, magical house was at stake.

CHAPTER 2

COLD WIND GUSTED AGAINST GEORGE'S FACE AS HE skated around the perimeter of the ice cream pond. The scent of sugar filled the air: the sweet, cold smell of the ice cream itself, and the warmer, even sweeter scent of the waffle cones baking in the stalls all around the pond. George could practically taste the cones at the back of his mouth. The wind might be cold, but George was warm enough from the skating that it wasn't bothering him. And besides —he inhaled deeply—it seemed like the ice cream stalls were handing out mostly chocolate ice cream today, so the wind wasn't really a bother.

He worked his tongue as he skated along, the closest stall just a score or so of paces up the snowy slope from the pond—and something tangled in his foot.

He smacked down hard on the ice cream surface.

Urgh. Ice cream it might be, but it was deep frozen.

It hurt.

George paused on his hands and knees for a moment, trying to sort out the scramble of sensations his body was throwing at him.

Knees, bruised.

Heels of his hands, grazed.

Calf muscle, aching.

Tongue, bleeding, filling his mouth with the metallic tang of blood where he'd bitten it on the left side as he'd come down.

"You okay?" Emma skished to a halt at his side, throwing up a tiny wave of ice cream chips—green and yellow in this part of the pond.

George spat blood from his mouth—and immediately regretted it. Spitting onto the ice cream surface felt sacrilegious somehow; even though it was literally a surface for skating on, it still felt too much like spitting into someone else's food.

And the bloodstain was vivid and out of place on the pastel-swirled surface of the pond.

"Yeah," he mumbled, twisting around to a sit and inspecting his knees. No grazing. No blood. He winced.

"I'm not sure how you think you're going to have a shot at the prize if you can't even keep your feet in training." Emma's tone was dismissive; she barely glanced down as George finished his inspection by rubbing at his knees.

George bit back a sharp retort. "Look, I know I'm not as good at this as Mabel," he said, scrubbing his hands through his hair and straining for politeness—he didn't want to jeopardise his sister's relationship with the best skating trainer in the state, after all—"but I swear that was not my fault. There was... something. I don't know." Confound the wind after all. He'd gotten so caught up in the taste of the chocolatey air that he'd... What? Not tripped on his own two feet, though it wouldn't have been the first time that had happened in his life. But this time, he was sure... "Isn't this surface supposed to be dead flat at all times?"

Emma narrowed her eyes. "What do you mean?"

George finished scrambling to his feet, brushing the frozen chips of lemon yellow and mint green from his knees. He cast about on the surface of the pond, a few paces back...

Ah, there.

Wincing, he skated to where he'd lost his balance, and crouched. He probed at the surface with increasingly confident fingers, lips pressing tighter and tighter together. "It's soft," he said as Emma joined him, her dark hair swinging down from under her white beanie, shielding her face.

She pressed a thumb against the swirl of pink ice cream and frowned as it left a slight impression. Slight —but it shouldn't have left any impression at all. "That's not right."

"What do we do?"

Her eyebrows lifted. "Do?" The look she turned on George had his insides writhing, but he refused to move or look away—even though his cheeks felt flaming hot. "We don't *do* anything," she said. "Well," she added, standing and brushing her hands off on her pristine white jacket, "you keep practising." She squinted at the sky, this late in the afternoon a pearly silver-grey of overcast clouds. "There's at least an hour until close. You've got a lot of ground to catch up."

George gritted his teeth. It wasn't *his* fault Mabel had always been the better skater. When Mum and Dad had first run into trouble a year or so back, there'd been only just enough money for *one* child to continue skating training. There'd been no question that it would be Mabel—and thank goodness she was as talented as she was, else she'd never have won the sponsorship from Ice Blades International, who'd been covering all her training costs for the last nine months—and had been giving her air time on their all-things-skating TV channel, too.

But... fine. Fine. George would keep practising, and let Emma—who clearly thought him too *unimportant* to have a conversation with about little things like the magically deep-frozen ice cream pond *melting*—deal with any other problems that arose.

Goodness knew he had enough problems on his plate right now anyway.

Sucking in a deep breath that smelled like waffle

cones and tasted like snow and blood, George spun away for another lap around the pond. Not half as elegantly as Mabel, of course—but it would do for now.

George tapped his fingers impatiently against the pen held idly in his other hand, frowning out his window (which, although closed, was currently emanating the distinct scent of baking apple pie). "I don't know," he said to Mabel, who was curled up in the lime-green beanbag on the floor of George's room, right leg in a space boot sticking awkwardly out in front of her. "I've never seen anything like it. It was soft, Mabes. Soft!"

Mabel, with eyes wide and serious, peered up at him where he perched restlessly on the edge of his bed. "And it tripped you up?"

He nodded, wincing at the sudden throb in his knees as he remembered his spectacular fall against the ice cream.

She frowned. "I wonder..."

His hands were stinging too, now that he thought about it—*so don't think about it, ignore them, it's just a bit of ice rash*—and his right knee in particular... "Hold on," he said. "What are you thinking?"

"When was the last time you saw me fall on the ice?" she said.

George opened his mouth and scrolled back through his mental calendar.

He shut his mouth. Pursed his lips. "Hmm," he said.

"Exactly." (There was a reason she'd been sponsored by Ice Blades International, after all.)

"So what are you saying?"

"I'm *saying,*" she said, leaning forward as far as she could without shifting her injured leg, "what if there was another soft patch?"

It was George's turn to frown. "Has anyone else seen one of these soft patches?" he asked.

Mabel shrugged. "No idea. No one's had any major falls recently though, so maybe this is just a new thing. Maybe it's never happened before. Maybe," she added, eyes lit up as she leaned forward again, "it's global warming, finally having an impact on the ice cream pond." She grinned.

George rolled his eyes. "Ridiculous." Mostly because the whole idea of a pond full of ice cream was ridiculous in the first place; if the Ice Cream Museum could defy nature to *make* the pond, he hardly thought something like global warming would be able to affect it.

Still. "Maybe I'll ask around tomorrow," he said. "See if anyone else has seen anything." It wouldn't hurt to figure out what was happening, if he could. If it didn't take away from his training.

CHAPTER 3

GEORGE HAD ASKED AROUND IN THE TWO DAYS FOLLOWING his fall, but no one else had seen or felt anything even approaching a soft patch in the ice. A couple of competitors looked worried at the prospect, telling George anxiously that they'd let him know if they saw anything. Most, though, simply shrugged and went about their business. Landon, the other favourite in the Junior Division, had laughed in George's face.

Now, three days later, George had been forced to push the whole thing from his mind; training was taking up his every spare minute, and he was too tired to even think about it. He ached from head to toe from using muscles he hadn't worked in months, and if it hadn't been for the fact that just this very morning he'd stuck his head out his window to discover that the whole backyard had been transformed from a square of concrete to a snow-drift of mint-coloured fairy floss, he might have been tempted to take more than his allotted fifteen minute mid-morning break right now.

As it was, he was bribing himself with the thought of the giant ice cream he'd get at lunchtime (the competitors didn't have to line up for the free ones like everybody else, they got two per day regardless), hopefully one of those incredible strawberry concoctions everyone seemed to be enjoying this morning, red-and-white ice cream piled precariously high on cones with red sauce made from real strawberries dripping down the sides and speckles of real vanilla throughout.

"Oof, sorry." George stepped back with a shudder from the man in the navy-blue pinstripe suit who, it seemed, had appeared without warning in front of him.

Then he frowned. If he'd known it was Max-From-The-Bank, he wouldn't have apologised.

Max glanced down at George dismissively with a twitch of his shoulders—and George was distracted from responding further by a wheezy voice crying out over the noise of the crowd from the gate to the skaters' area.

"But it's just not safe!"

George rolled his eyes. It was Avi again, arguing with one of the skating pond marshals who lolled against the sheep-panel fence, making sure only competitors, their coaches, and registered support people made it through the gate. The other day it had been unsafe potholes, and now, apparently, there was something unsafe about the Ice Cream Crown Skating Races themselves.

Lungs full of the ice-cold air (even mid-morning the temperatures were brisk), nose full of the scent of waffle cones even though it was barely time for brunch (but 'waffle cones' had the word 'waffle' in it, so they were clearly a breakfast food), George joined the short queue of contestants lined up on the slushy ground, waiting to enter the competitors' zone. He was fully prepared to ignore Avi (*focus on training, must do better in my take-off, I'm losing time there*)—until Avi made a final strangled sound and whirled away from the marshal, practically elbowing George in the nose.

George hissed, clapping his hands over a nose that now streamed blood. His eyes teared up involuntarily as pain spiked through him.

"There!" Avi said emphatically, gesturing no less wildly than the flail that had caused the injury in the first place. "You see? Dangerous."

Through tear-blurred eyes and still hunched over, George squinted up at Avi. "I hardly think," he said, then paused to wince as pain lanced through his face again. He sucked a shaky breath in through his mouth. "It's not the skating that's dangerous." He'd've liked to glare at Avi harder, but it was difficult to appear really angry when both your eyes and your nose insisted on leaking.

"Here, here." It was Mabel, hobbling along with crutches in the space boot—the ankle had been a minor fracture, not a serious break, though it'd be enough to keep her in the boot for a couple of months—and pulling his hands away so she could shove a wadded up blue handkerchief at him to soak up the blood.

George jerked away as she pressed too hard, but took the handkerchief and began gently mopping at his face.

"Are you still okay to train?" Two vertical lines creased Mabel's forehead above her nose.

George glanced down to the pastel-swirled pond. Emma was already out there waiting, easy to spot in her snow-white jacket, arms folded and probably a scowl on her face, though he couldn't quite tell that from this distance.

Through an inhalation that smelled and tasted of blood, George nodded. "Emma'll have my head if I don't."

Mabel squeezed his arm. "Take it easy, okay?"

He nodded, but the races were barely two days away. Now was really not the time for taking things easy if he was going to have even a *chance* at winning.

The metallic tang of blood still overpowering the sweet, sugary smells in the air, George made his way down through the slushy snow to the edge of the pond and put his skates on. If he shoved the anxiety aside for just a moment—over the races, over the house—he could remember just how great it was to be back out on the ice (cream) again doing regular training after so long. Even the aches and complaints of his muscles felt familiar now that he was out here.

He hadn't said anything at the time, because what would have been the point, but giving up skating that year or so ago had been one of the most heart-breaking things he'd done in his fourteen years of existence.

Nothing beat the feel of the air whipping past as you made a full speed run down the length of the pond; the perfect balance of a fast spin; the sound of skates shishing on the ice as you executed a perfect hockey stop.

George glided out to where Emma waited for him, right in the very centre of the pond atop a five-pointed swirl of mint-green.

(Not that it tasted anything like mint, of course. George—like everyone else who'd ever skated on the ice cream, except maybe Emma because she seemed too serious for that sort of thing—had of course sampled the flavours of the different colours in the pond, just a furtive swipe of a finger over the smooth, icy surface before quickly licking it, just to see. The colours all tasted the same, though, a generic sweet flavour that was probably supposed to be caramel.)

Sure enough, Emma tapped her long, olive fingers against one elbow and frowned. "Think you can hold yourself together long enough to avoid yet another injury?"

George held his tongue and simply nodded, but really, 'another' injury? He'd tripped *once* in the two weeks they'd been training, and his current face-mess was hardly his fault.

Emma narrowed her eyes as though hearing his thoughts. After a moment, though, she waved her hand toward an empty patch of ice. "Spins first," she said. "Then we'll practise your starts some more. At least you have speed," she added under her breath as George took off toward the palace she'd indicated; he wasn't sure he'd been supposed to hear that last bit at all.

He executed the first three spins perfectly, elbows in tight, ankles crossed, rotating so fast the world blurred around him.

The fourth time, he leapt into the spin—and his left skate went out from underneath him.

George smacked down on the rock-hard ice cream.

Air burst from his lungs. He gasped, chest tight.

His elbow burned where he'd smacked it on the ice, and his left knee was going to have a heck of a bruise.

For a second, he let his head sag against the ice, close enough that the sweet smell overpowered the lingering blood in his sinuses.

Two days. He had only two days left until the races, and what if he'd done himself some serious damage now? It was going to hurt to get up, he could tell, and what if it was bad enough that he wouldn't recover in time?

His fists curled against the ice, frustrating knotting in his stomach.

Behind him, someone shished to a stop.

"Hmm." It was Emma, and the speculation in her tone was enough to make George sit up and turn around.

She should have been mad at him, not thoughtful.

But she was staring at a patch of blue ice cream as though she could incinerate it—or perhaps freeze it even more solid—with her gaze alone.

"What is it?"

She glanced up at him. "Another soft spot."

George frowned.

In response, Emma only inclined her head, indicating the blue ice cream at her feet.

George scrambled up—yep, he'd been right, the knee was a killer, but it seemed like it hadn't been *seriously* damaged—and skated over.

A soft patch, easily visible now the sun was climbing higher in the sky, the surface a little too shiny to look at, lacking the solid crust of frost that the rest of the pond had.

George bent down to touch it—and jerked his hand away almost immediately. The spot was easily soft enough to take the impression of his thumb. And that was seriously, seriously Not Good. "What do we do?" he said, more urgently than last time. If she ignored him again, if she told him to just get on with practice...

But her brow furrowed, dark eyes narrowing. "Stay here," she said. "We need to mark the place." She turned and zipped away, heading for the entry ramp—and the race officials.

Barely a minute or two later she returned, this time with Audrey (head of the racing committee, known by her first name only) skating along beside her, Audrey's blue eyes filled with the same worry that Emma was mostly doing a good job of hiding.

George pursed his lips as he spotted Avi in tow behind them both, grim determination on his face. How he'd nagged his way out onto the ice right now was anybody's guess, and George's stomach flip-flopped at the thought of all the complaints Avi might be able to make now about the 'safety' of the races.

The three of them stopped, making a ring around the soft spot with George, and peered down at the offending blue ice cream.

"Trying to bribe the officials?"

George whirled around as his competitor Landon whipped past, blond curls flying out from under his red knitted beanie, a grin plastered on his pale face as he turned effortlessly and skated backward so he could taunt George without slowing down.

George scowled at him and turned away—but not before he saw Landon execute a perfect triple spin and sprint away toward the other side of the pond.

If George hadn't been so worried about the ice cream softening, Landon's performance just now might have had his stomach doing flips regardless.

Landon had started skating around the same time George had, and they'd never been friendly, and had always been neck and neck in any show of skill.

And Landon hadn't had a year-long break from training.

Another string of complaints from Avi drew George's attention back to the matter at hand. "I told you! I told you it wasn't safe!" Avi was saying, practically tugging on Audrey's metallic-silver sleeve. "The whole thing should be shut down immediately!"

George could practically sense Audrey trying not to roll her eyes. "Avi," she said, not unkindly, "a moment ago you were telling me it's not safe because of the crowds, and before that you were complaining that all the sugar is bad for people. I get that you're not a fan of the races, but at this point I'm going to have to ask you to head on over to the Museum and lodge a formal complaint—if you can narrow it down to just one—and leave the area before I report you for harassment."

George barely suppressed a snort, and even Emma pressed her lips tightly together as though hiding a smile.

Avi, however, clenched his teeth tightly and seemed about to burst. He whirled away, muttering. "See this contest closed," George caught as the man glided past. "Unnatural..." The rest of his complaints were lost to distance.

George stared after him and shook his head.

"Yes, he tripped on another one last week," Emma said, and George realised Audrey had asked about the other soft spot he'd found. "He does seem to have a knack for it."

What?! A knack for tripping over things? That was hardly fair!

...But then again, maybe she'd only meant he had a knack for finding soft spots. And that was a very different matter.

Because maybe it was entirely coincidental...

"No one else has seen any?" he asked softly.

Audrey shook her head, fair hair swinging in its ponytail, a frown creasing her similarly fair face. "This is the first I've heard of it," she said.

George's stomach twisted.

...Or maybe it wasn't a coincidence at all that he was the only person on the pond finding soft spots.

Maybe—just maybe—someone wanted him out of the competition.

Across the pond, Landon executed another perfect triple and skated out of the spin with almost eye-blurring speed.

George pursed his lips. *Now, who on earth could want me out of the competition, I wonder?*

No points for guessing that.

CHAPTER 4

GEORGE'S SKATES BUMPED GENTLY AGAINST THE SNOW at the edge of the pond, and he frowned as Mabel came hobbling to greet him.

"What's wrong?" she said, brow furrowed with concern. "I saw you fall, and then Audrey and Avi, and you were all standing around looking at the ice cream. Was there—"

"—another soft patch." George nodded. "Yeah."

Mabel's frown deepened. "But still no one else has seen any?"

He shook his head as he plunked down onto the nearest bench and began removing his skates.

Mabel dropped his shoes near his feet and sat next to him, the black space boot sticking out in front of her.

Wind gusted past, bringing a tangle of fruity scents that had a strong berry component.

"I think someone's doing this deliberately."

George pulled his second skate off with a little more force than strictly necessary.

Mabel shifted, leaning forward on her wrists. "But *how*? I just don't see *how* anyone could be doing this on purpose." She pursed her lips and exhaled.

George pulled his shoes on, tugged the laces tight, and snatched up his skates. Only ten or fifteen paces away to his right, a certain figure in their bright red jacket was skating up to the shore. "I don't know," George said, eyes on Landon as he did the awkward skates-on-shore hobble to the wooden bench closest to him. "But maybe that's the wrong way to look at it. Maybe we need to figure out *who* is doing it first, and *then* we can figure out how."

Mabel followed George's gaze. Her already pursed lips became even thinner. "Be careful," she said softly, for George's ears only. "Don't pick a fight."

George cut her a sharp glance. "I'm not going to do anything stupid."

But that was a good point, really. What *was* he going to do?

Landon had unlaced his skates in record time and was already gathering his things to leave.

Abruptly, George made his decision. "I'm going to follow him," he muttered to Mabel. "See if I can find anything."

Mabel's eyes widened, but she didn't say anything.

George took that as all the agreement he was likely to get and shoved his yellow jacket on as quickly as he could.

"Wait," Mabel interrupted as he went to leave. "Give me that." She gestured impatiently at his jacket.

George's brow furrowed.

She tossed her head impatiently. "It's too bright. You'll literally stand out in the crowd. You want to be stealthy, don't you?"

"Right." George stripped back out of the jacket and passed it to Mabel.

"Here." She handed him her pastel pink one, and he took it with a shrug. It *was* far too cold to be without a jacket, and Landon definitely wouldn't recognise him in pastel pink.

"Much better." Mabel gave a nod as she appraised him critically, then jerked her head at the gate. "Better hurry."

George slushed through the trampled snow up the slope to the gate, searching this way and that for Landon's distinctive red jacket.

Ah, there. Not far to the right, almost at the closest ice cream stall. George hurried to catch up, then followed a bit behind, far enough that once or twice his stomach twisted as he lost Landon in the crush and press of the crowd. But each time, George darted around the person who'd gotten between them—usually someone holding one of the towering strawberry confections the stalls were serving today—and spotted Landon just ahead in his bright red jacket and matching beanie, blond curls sticking out around the rim.

They wound through the chattering, jostling people, heading steadily to the western end of the pond, and as Landon left the main body of the crowd and joined the constant stream of people heading west, George realised. The Ice Cream Museum. That's where Landon was heading.

George pursed his lips—and turned abruptly aside as Landon glanced around. He could practically *feel* Landon's gaze slide right over him. Thank goodness he'd taken Mabel's jacket after all. From the corner of his eye, he watched until Landon resumed his slightly furtive walk before turned back to face the Museum.

As they drew closer, the three storeys of the Museum seemed to rear out of the snow like a giant rainbow. Painted in pastel shades of blue and pink and yellow, the building seemed more like something you'd expect in an amusement park than in the middle of a fairly neat and old-fashioned large town. But it was a pretty amazing piece of architecture, columns out the front twisting and spiralling like ice cream piled on a cone, the roof three storeys up hammered bronze that gleamed in the winter sunlight, textured to look like a giant piece of waffle cone.

Landon vanished into the entrance, and a moment later, George followed.

Or tried to: instead, a full-body shudder ran through him as someone burst out through the doors, nearly knocking George off his feet.

He slipped on the slushy snow at the edge of the concrete path, caught himself—and scowled at Max-From-The-Bank's back as he stormed off back toward the ice cream pond.

What on earth was he doing here? George didn't exactly pick him for the kind of whimsical person who usually visited the Museum. Maybe he was a history buff, they liked museums—right? George frowned. None of that explained why he'd been so angry, though.

The frown turned back to a scowl. Why was he wasting time trying to figure out the inner workings of the man who was literally trying to take away George's slightly magical home?

George snorted, brushed himself off, and headed into the Ice Cream Museum.

Of course, by now Landon was nowhere to be seen. He might've continued on the main floor, through the exhibition of the history of ice cream flavours (complete with scratch-and-sniff experiences), or he might've gone upstairs to the history of the Skating Races, or to the top floor with its generic information on the history of ice cream itself. No way to know.

George took a deep breath—the air in here was warm and dry, with faint traces of vanilla.

An angry voice echoed out across the general chatter of the scattering of patrons in the foyer with its waffle-cone coloured tiles.

Avi, over at the ticket and information desk, which had been done up to look like a charming, old-fashioned ice cream store, done in shades of cream and blue. Audrey had told Avi to take his complaints to the Museum, and obviously that's exactly what he was doing, gesticulating wildly at the poor young man currently staffing the desk.

George rolled his eyes and, for no reason other than to get away from the arguing as quickly as possible, took the stairs up to the next floor.

The wide stairs began at the end of the foyer, heading straight up before branching in two half-way up. The curling, twisting banister rail had been gilded and textured with a waffle pattern; it felt cool and pleasant under George's palm as he climbed. He took the right branch of stairs, then turned right again at the top, where a short hallway opened out into a room divided into a kind of twisting maze by floor-to-ceiling panels of frosted glass.

Little blue lights were set into the floor and roof periodically, sparkling off the glass and giving the whole room the appearance of the inside of an ice palace. Somehow the air even smelled of ice, despite the fact that the temperature was pleasant enough. Quite pretty, really, this room detailing the life history of the Snow Queen—such as it was known, anyway.

George rounded a corner of the glass-walled maze—and nearly bumped into a woman about his height, fair-skinned with a halo of curls that were probably light brown, though it was a little hard to tell in the frost-blue lighting of the room. He shivered. "Sorry," George said, shifting his weight so he didn't bump her.

The woman shivered visibly, but she turned to him and smiled, the kind of smile that went right to your bones and made you feel like things would be okay. "Hello," she said. "Are you just visiting?"

George smiled back, and even though it was a bit strained around the edges he felt like this kindly woman probably wouldn't mind. "I was looking for someone," he said. "I'm from the Races."

Her eyebrows lifted. "A racer? Well. How exciting. Which division do you race in?"

"Oh, uh, the Junior Division," George said, his cheeks warming. "I mean, I wasn't really supposed to be, my sister, she's the favourite, but she fell, and I didn't want us to lose the house so I took her place, and..." He stopped short, cheeks fairly burning now. "Sorry."

"I'm Mat," the woman said with a slow nod. Her eyebrows had settled back into their places, but her eyes still sparkled in the strange silver-and-blue lighting of the glass-walled maze. "Nice to meet you."

"George," he said, drawing in a deep, calming breath. A suspicion tickled the back of his mind. "You don't..." He cast a quick glance over her clothing: waffle-coloured slacks and a baby-blue polo shirt. "I don't suppose you work here, do you?"

Her smile deepened. "You could say that, yes."

George took another long breath, this time a breath of preparation. "You don't know anything that would cause patches of the ice cream pond to melt at all, do you?"

The frown that creased Mat's face was instant and intense. "Melt? Is this a hypothetical question, or have you seen something?"

The urgency in her tone rocked George back on his heels a little. "I, uh, um, yeah. No. It's not hypothetical. I fell," he hurried on as her stare intensified. "And so did my sister. And there were soft patches in the ice cream. At least, there were the two times I fell, I'm not sure about my sister, but given she was supposed to win the races she's that good and the last time I saw her fell I can't even remember—"

Mat held up a hand. "Magic," she said simply, and George's brow wrinkled for a moment. "The only thing that could cause the ice cream to melt is magic, and fairly strong magic, too."

The air conditioning shifted gears and a waft of cooler, ice-scented air drifted past, ruffling Mat's curls and setting George shivering. "The Snow Queen?" he asked.

Mat shook her head. "No, not her."

"Then who?" Landon? Surely not, if there was magic involved...

"There is one other like the Snow Queen, maybe two. And some people..." She tilted her head at him and an echo of her earlier smile crept back into her eyes. "Some people can be taught."

George's lips pursed. Right. So it might still be Landon then. "It could be anyone then," he said.

"No." Her curls bounced as she shook her head again. "Very *few* people can be taught."

It still might be Landon.

In his thoughts, George constructed the visuals of a scenario where Landon snuck into the Museum every day to stalk the Snow Queen and learn her secrets, which he could then use to wipe out his competitors on the pond. The Landon in his imagination was a little taller than the real Landon, and had a disconcerting tendency to cackle—but the point remained. It *could* be Landon.

George glanced back up at Mat.

She was still watching him, something knowing in her expression.

The skin on his back crawled.

"I, uh, thanks," he said quickly. "That's... that's really helpful." He backed away. Landon could be following the Snow Queen right now, watching her, learning her secrets. "I, uh... I have to go find that person. Thanks."

He turned as soon as it seemed polite, and practically ran from the room, Mat's strange, piercing gaze making his shoulder blades itch all the while.

CHAPTER 5

ALACK, GEORGE HAD MISSED HIS OPPORTUNITY TO LEARN anything more about Landon that day: he'd appeared in the foyer again right as George had reached the top of the stairs, hands full of brochures of some sort, heading back to the pond.

George hadn't been able to see what the brochures were, and following Landon around for the next three days had also failed to reveal anything—but then again, neither had George found any more soft spots.

Not, that was, until the day of the races themselves.

George had won his heat easily the day before—Emma had been so pleased she'd actually smiled at him, and Mabel had just about squished him in half—and had secured himself a place in the Junior Division semi-finals, scheduled for the morning program on the big official day of the races (his final would be in the afternoon). And it was the big official day right enough: the crowd around the pond had thickened so that George was intensely grateful for the railed off walkway allowing contes-tants access to the pond; it might have taken him more than ten minutes of concerted pushing and shoving to make it to the gate otherwise. As it was, a whole bunch of pushing and shoving seemed to be going on as people vied for the best views of the pond. Some enterprising person had set up a small grandstand of white wooden bleachers a way back from the pond and was charging people ten bucks each to grab a seat where they could see right over the heads of everyone else, straight down to the pastel-swirled pond.

Even more enterprising, George noted with a sniff and pursed lips, was the extra fifty bucks to borrow a pair of binoculars. That was especially amusing when he spotted Bank-Max on the top tier of the seating. George's sniff turned to an outright snort; no doubt with all the money Max made repossessing houses, sixty bucks to sit on a chair with a pair of glorified eye goggles seemed like barely a pittance. And besides, Max'd be so used to lording it over other people he probably wouldn't survive if he wasn't seated high over everyone else's heads.

Josef nodded George through the gate into the competitors' preparation area.

George shoved Max, the bank, and the house

from his mind, inhaling and exhaling firmly.

The scent of waffle cones seemed supercharged today; the air was practically warm with it, the sweet smell winding its way over crowds and lingering in coat folds and locks of hair. People would smell of it for days after, the same way the scent of an open fire was carried away by the people who gathered at it to catch in the nose for days afterward, no matter how thoroughly you washed your hair.

Not that the waffle cone smell was bad—or that woodsmoke was, really, come to think of it; it reminded George of home, of the fireplace in their front lounge room, of long winter nights curled up by the crackling flames with family, in a place where he belonged—*No, stop, don't think about the house, not now, not yet*—but it was *persistent*. And, combined with the butterflies zipping about in George's stomach, the effect was somewhat nauseating.

He pressed a hand against his stomach as he perched on a bench, in the middle of lacing his skates, and swallowed hard against the sour burn in the back of his throat.

"You'll be fine," Mabel said encouragingly. But he knew her well enough to spot the lingering fear at the outer corners of her eyes, that little tightness that meant she was worried too, the redness around the rim of the inner corners that indicated she'd slept as poorly last night as he had.

Beside Mabel, Emma pursed her lips and flipped

her dark hair—at least as well as hair could be flipped when it was mostly contained by a knitted white beanie that sparkled with silver thread in the morning sunlight.

A fresh breeze gusted across the pond, bringing the scent of deep-frozen ice cream—more muted than the waffle cones, colder, icier, with that subtle caramel undertone—and instinct pulled George's gaze to the far horizon. He frowned. "Hope it doesn't rain."

Mabel followed his gaze. "I wouldn't hold that hope too deeply," she muttered.

The wind picked up as though in answer, bearing the deep grey-blue clouds closer and bringing with them the smell of rain. It was almost enough to quench the sugaryness of the air—almost, but not quite. George could still taste waffle cone at the back of his throat.

A ripple ran through the crowd, across the pond to the left. A small bubble seemed to be opening around someone, hidden for now by the press of the crowd—but the silence begun by that ripple seemed to spread, and even George and his companions fell silent, watching intently, George with the laces of his left skate still firmly in hand.

A woman approached the fence, visible now as the crowd parted around her: on the shorter side of average, with a halo of light brown curls around a face that seemed kindly, like at any moment she might choose to smile, her eyes shining with a light that said she was poised on the brink of reaching out to you to smooth your cheek, pat your shoulder, offer a kind word and quietly but inexorably light up your life just a tiny bit more than it had been. She gave out a soft light, not quite like she was glowing—or perhaps like she was, but only if you glanced sideways at her.

The rest of the world seemed bleak by comparison.

Even the ice cream pond seemed somehow less fantastical, colours somehow muted, as the woman strode out onto the ice without skates, only snow-white sneakers with her jeans, and an ice-blue hoodie.

George couldn't shake the feeling that she seemed vaguely familiar, and not just because she was the Snow Queen.

The wind gusted again, this time spitting cold sleet into people's faces.

George winced, wiped absently at his cheek—but didn't take his eyes off the woman now in the centre of the pond.

Neither, it seemed, had the rest of the crowd. Silence reigned as she lifted her hands toward the inclement clouds. For a moment, it seemed as though a silver-and-crystal crown rested upon her head. She made a complicated gesture that reminded George of folding clothes, tucking bit in here and turning parts over there...

And a beam of sunlight shot down through the clouds, opening a rift in the centre of them right above the pond of frozen ice cream.

The mint green and baby pink, lemon yellow and bubblegum blue brightened like a rainbow.

The woman repeated the complicated series of folding gestures and the rift in the clouds opened wider.

Rain began to fall in earnest now—but it didn't touch the pond, or the fence around it, or the crowds...

In fact, George estimated the rift in clouds to be five hundred paces or so now, bright blue sky shining through. Some of the nausea in his stomach dimmed. It was, in fact, a perfect day for skating right now, at least over the pond where it mattered—and he couldn't wait to get racing.

CHAPTER 6

THE BUTTERFLIES IN GEORGE'S STOMACH HAD SETTLED into a steady rhythm as he'd watched the Open Division run-outs, races for everyone who hadn't made it through to the Open semi-finals so they could still race on the official day of the carnival and get some experience under race conditions.

The Races were divided into three age categories: Tinies (for the under tens), Juniors (ages ten through fourteen) and the Open division, for anyone old enough to keep up. By regular ice skating standards, it made no sense—but George had always supposed sense to be too much to ask for when it came to races literally skated on ice cream.

All three of the divisions raced the same distance, the Tinies obviously taking a lot longer to do so—but the Ice Cream Crown Skating Races were about more than simply speed. Not only did competitors have to race three times around the pond, they also had to navigate a series of obstacles like the Boysenberry Ripple tunnel, and the Chocolate Twirl spin. And the obstacles were what really set the Junior division above the Tinies in terms of difficulty, and the Open ahead of them both.

The last of the Open run-outs was just finishing up now, and from his seat on a bench in the competitors' preparation area, George tensed, leaning forward with eyes eagle-focused on the distinctive bright-pink band of the finish line as an Open competitor—a woman in a navy-blue racing suit—whipped across. The crowd cheered, and beside him, Mabel did too.

"Stella usually trains around the same time I do," she said to George by way of explanation. "She's very generous with her tips and tricks. She's the one who helped me finally crack the Boysenberry Ripple. I'm surprised she didn't make it to the semis, actually."

George nodded seriously and added some polite applause.

But what he was mostly thinking of was the fact that the steady, rhythmic butterflies of adrenalin in his stomach were going to make it extremely hard to eat or even drink anything, but that he should probably try, because now that the Open run outs were over, there was only the Tinies semi-finals to go before his own semi-finals race.

As if summoned by his thoughts, Emma appeared, dark hair contained by her usual white-and-silver knitted beanie, her white jacket looking pristine as ever. "Here," she said, and shoved a bottle of something blue at him. "Drink."

He took the bottle, cold against his palm, but didn't realise he was sitting and staring at it until Mabel nudged him. "You'd better drink," she murmured.

George nodded. He gulped down a mouthful, wondering if he'd get lucky and it would drown the butterflies. It was some sort of energy drink, sweet and tasting of fake berries. He pulled a face at the overly sweet taste, but dutifully sculled down half the bottle before setting it aside.

It must have been enough, at least for now, because Emma nodded approvingly and strode away again, leaving George's gaze wandering out over the pond to where the Tinies were lining up for their semis.

Unsurprisingly, most of the kids who'd made it this far were on the older side of the age bracket, though there was one kid—of indeterminate gender at this distance—who was surprisingly short. Someone who hadn't hit a growth spurt yet, or genuinely a younger competitor for a change? Mentally, George wished them luck and hoped it boded well for his race; he'd only just turned fourteen a month ago, and he knew at least three of the people he'd be up against in the semis were getting close to fifteen.

Mind you, he thought, *Mabel was one of the prime favourites, and she's only twelve. So.*

The Tinies race was over all too soon—the notably short competitor had made it through to the finals, good for them—and George was lining up behind the blue starting line, other competitors jostling him on either side as they all vied for the best starting position. There were no lanes in this race, just the course ahead of them, and if you weren't in a good position when you hit the first obstacle, it was nearly impossible to claw back enough speed to make it through to the next round.

George's heart hammered at his chest, the blue energy drink joining the butterflies in doing somersaults, even though it had had forty minutes to digest.

A pity the butterflies couldn't be similarly digested.

George pursed his lips as Landon jostled his way to George's right side, grinning at him from under his bright-red beanie. "May the best competitor win," Landon said, which sounded generous unless you knew that, without a doubt, he meant himself.

George did his best to ignore him, adjusting his footing slightly. The starts were always his downfall, and apart from spins, they were what Landon did best. If Landon got too much of a jump on him...

But the starter was calling out, and a tension fell

over the competitors, muscles taut, eyes straining, mouths pressed into lines of focus.

Crack. The starter's gun whipped them into motion.

George leapt forward, centre of gravity low, pushing off just like Emma had been coaching him. Shish, shish, shish, faster, faster across the icy surface.

The first obstacle loomed.

Landon was going to beat him there, but otherwise George had a clean shot at it: the Boysenberry Ripple, a shoulder-high tunnel that rippled left and right for about ten metres. He ducked, swerved left, right, left, right... Emerged right on Landon's tail.

He'd left the butterflies behind in the tunnel.

Here, now, ahead of the rest of the field, there was only the ice cream, swirling below his feet as his skates carved across it, the rhythm matching his breaths.

The second obstacle, the third... George nailed them both, hot on Landon's heels the whole time.

Skish, skish. Shish, shish.

Breathe in, breathe out.

Left, right, spin, the ice cream spraying up a little as he landed.

George headed into the Chocolate Twirl obstacle only a pace behind Landon. He braced to spin—and something smacked him, hard, in the face, the arm, the hip...

At first he thought he'd fallen again by himself.

But a sharp groan from behind him sounded.

Landon. *Landon* had fallen, and, hot on his heels, George had tripped over *Landon*.

Numb, not really sure what he was feeling (apart from sore—he massaged his left shoulder), George clambered to his feet.

Landon hadn't started getting up yet.

George's gaze flickered to the Chocolate Twirl.

He and Landon had made it through in practically record time, and the next competitor was only just reaching it. If he took off again now, he could probably still win.

Landon's face was twisted in pain.

Gritting his teeth, George skated over to where Landon had fallen. "You okay?" he said, offering his hand.

Landon stared up at him, eyebrows lifting. "What are you doing? You could be winning!"

Jaw still tight, George waggled his hand impatiently. "We both could be."

Landon rolled his eyes, but accepted George's hand and scrambled to his feet—as the next competitor skated past, and the next. "Fool," Landon muttered—and stumbled, nearly pulling George down again.

George clutched at him, trying to steady them both—and gasped. "Is that..."

He bent down, one arm still holding onto Landon, and pressed his fingertips against the lemon-yellow swirl.

A soft patch. Another one, and this time it had tripped Landon up.

"It wasn't you," George said, not meaning to sound quite as disbelieving as he did and hoping desperately that Landon wouldn't notice.

"What wasn't me?"

George pressed his fingertips harder against the ice cream surface, hardly caring at all that half the field had now passed them by. "Look," he said. "The ice cream. It's soft."

A deep frown creasing his face, Landon bent to touch the slightly squishy, slightly melted section of yellow ice cream. "But, it can't do that."

"This is why I fell those other times," George said, feeling just a touch smug that now Landon would have to believe him.

Landon only blinked, staring at the ice cream oozing up around his fingertips.

He stood abruptly. "Someone has to do something," he said.

George nodded, straightening also. "We have to go tell the officials," he said.

Landon nodded, absently wiping his sticky fingers on George's sleeve. "Maybe they'll let us rerun the race once they see what happened."

George pursed his lips as Landon took off, cutting across the pond off course, straight toward the official's tent that stood, bright blue, next to the red medic's one on the far side of the pond by the skaters' marshalling area.

But he followed, a tiny seed of hope thinking

about maybe sprouting.

If Landon was right… If the officials could be convinced to rerun the race… George thought of the house, of his parents watching from shore, of Mabel watching from the competitors' area.

The seed of hope became a slurry of worms writhing in his belly. They had to let him try again. They just had to.

CHAPTER 7

"WHAT HAPPENED?" EMMA DEMANDED AS GEORGE skated back to the competitors' area. "Why did you fall?"

"Was it Landon?" Mabel asked earnestly, coming to meet him as he stepped off the ice cream, glaring over his shoulder as Landon glided in behind, favouring his left knee a little.

George nodded. "Yeah, but it's not what you think. There was another soft patch," he added, meeting Emma's gaze.

"Right," she said, face tightening. "That's it."

She whirled and stomped away—directly toward the officials' tent.

George watched her go for a moment, then shook his head. "I'm sorry, Mabes," he said, stomach twisting and he turned back to her. He shivered. The wind had picked up, and now that he wasn't hyped up on nerves or skating full pelt across the pond, he was starting to cool. The scent of waffle cones still hung heavy in the air, still turning his stomach, which was no longer knotting from nerves, but instead from disappointment. "The house..."

Mabel flung her arms around him and squeezed him tightly. "Oh George. I know. But you did your best, what else can we do?"

"I'm sorry," he whispered, hugging her back.

"Don't be sorry," Landon said from behind George, voice overly loud and obnoxious. "They'll *have* to let us run it again. There's no way this is fair."

George squashed down the hope that threatened to rise again as Emma came striding up again, this time leading Audrey.

"You said there was another soft patch?" A small frown tugged at the corners of Audrey's mouth and eyes as she herself tugged at the hem of her glittering silver jacket, the cold air reddening her pale cheeks.

George nodded. "Right before the Chocolate Twirl."

"Do you think you could find it again?" said Audrey.

"Well obviously," Landon said, rolling his eyes. "It'll be where all the scraping is from the fall."

"I know exactly where it is," George added. He'd made sure of that before he'd left the pond, scanning in all directions for landmarks so he'd be able to find his way back to the place exactly.

"Show me." Audrey gestured to the pond, now almost empty as everyone headed off for lunch. "If we can find evidence of tampering..."

Hope thrilled through George like adrenalin on fire. If they could find evidence... Was Landon right after all? Did that mean they'd rerun the race? That he might have a shot at the finals after all?

Practically skating as fast as in the actual races, George and Landon led Audrey and Emma out to the place on the pond where they'd fallen; Landon got there first and cast around uselessly for a moment, but George skated right to the place, exactly aligned between the entrance to the Chocolate Twirl, a distinctive swirl of pastel blue ice cream, and the western-most ice cream stand up at the fence where the crowd still milled, the noise of their chatter like a distant river in the background. "It was right... here..." George said, frowning at the ice cream surface which was completely flat, smooth... and entirely un-soft.

Audrey cocked an eyebrow. "Are you sure?" she asked. "It might be quite hard to find again..."

George shook his head firmly. "I know—"

"Look!" Landon said, cutting him off. "See? All this scraping? That's where I tripped," he said, face flushed —with anger or just adrenalin, George couldn't tell.

"I'm not saying you're wrong," Audrey said slowly as Emma's eyes flashed anger at George. "But... there doesn't seem to be any evidence here of a soft patch now, does there?" She spread her hands at the ground and shrugged a little helplessly.

"But you saw us fall!" George said. "You saw!"

Audrey shrugged again. "Falls happen. Who's to say he didn't just trip, and you got too close behind him?"

George's chest grew tight and he balled his hands into fists at his sides, his cheeks heating enough that he knew he'd be just as red now as Landon. Audrey's tone was verging on defensive, and if she didn't outright think the boys were lying, she certainly wasn't rushing to believe them. "There was a soft spot," George said through teeth that felt too tightly clenched. "Just like those times in training," he added, glaring at Emma. Why wasn't she saying something to back them up?

"There really was," Landon insisted. "I touched it and everything. Look," he added. "He's my biggest competitor." He pointed at George. "Why would I team up with him on... anything?"

"I'm sorry," Audrey said, and to her credit she did look genuinely sorry. "But without factual evidence, there's really very little I can do." She offered them a sympathetic smile, and swished away.

Emma's glare intensified. "How dare you," she said in a tight voice.

George recoiled; that was not what he'd been expecting from her at all.

But it was on Landon that she rounded. "No

reason for you to team up? None? I don't know about you," she snapped, eyes bright as lightning, "but if I fell down in the semis and tangled up the other top contender as I went, I'd feel pretty darn embarrassed. Both favourites, falling in the quals?"

George's stomach flip-flopped, mostly because she was mad, but also... She'd considered him a favourite to win too? He hadn't realised that.

"Much better to cook up some rubbish story about a soft patch so you'd both have an excuse. And you!" She whirled back to George now, and he shrank away. "You've made me look like a complete fool. Don't think I don't know this was your idea. Soft patch. Soft patch indeed!" Emma shook her head and skated off, arms tightly folded over her ribs.

George's chest ached. His throat ached. Surely Emma had to believe him. She had to! It wasn't a random accident, there'd been another soft patch, and if she didn't believe him...

His throat tightened. That was it, then. The house was gone.

Dully, George skated back to the shore where Mabel waited expectantly.

"What?" she asked as soon as he was within earshot without her having to shout over the mutterings from the crowd. "What happened?"

"It's gone," he said, dropping heavily onto the bench and bending to remove his skates. He rubbed at the tip of his nose with his shoulder to try to warm it a little.

Nothing at all to do with the fact that his eyes felt prickly.

"The soft patch?" Mabel said quietly as she sat beside him.

George nodded. The noise of the crowd washed around him, drifting down from the fence with the smell of warm sugar.

The soft patch was gone, his chance at the finals was gone... And their house. Also gone.

"How would you even make a soft patch like that?"

George glanced up abruptly; he'd been so caught up in his own thoughts that he hadn't realised Landon had followed him.

Landon continued without waiting for a response. "Like, what did someone do? Carry a thermos of boiling water and dump it on the ice?"

"Ha ha," George said. "Sure. I'm skating along, right in the middle of the semi-finals, competitor hot on my heels, and I'm just going to take a second to whip out this thermos of hot water I've been conveniently hiding on my person and spill it all over the ground without anyone noticing." He gave Landon a pointed look, eyebrows a little raised. "And quite besides anything else, there'd be splash marks. The patches were perfectly round."

Landon shrugged. "Okay genius, you tell me how they're happening."

"Magic," George said grimly as he tugged his skates off.

Landon's eyebrows shot up. "Magic?"

George nodded. "I talked to someone at the Museum the other day. They said the only way someone could interfere with the ice cream like that was magic. I..." George stared down at the skates now in his hands. "I thought it might have been you, actually."

Laughter burst out of Landon like sunlight shooting out from behind a cloud—not the pretty kind, the blinding kind that made you squint and wince and hope the clouds would come back in a hurry so you could actually see again.

George rolled his eyes, passed his skates to Mabel for a moment, and pulled on his boots.

"Okay," said Landon. "But seriously. Any ideas about who would want to interfere with the races like this?"

George pulled the last knot on his laces tight with more force than necessary. He stood. "No," he said. "But I know where we need to go to find out."

CHAPTER 8

MABEL HAD INSISTED ON COMING WITH GEORGE AND Landon, which George thought was fair enough seeing as she'd probably been the first person to trip over a soft patch in the ice cream pond, but on the other hand made the journey up through the crowds and down the road to the Museum rather slower than it would have been otherwise.

Landon kept having to visibly adjust his pace, and George was torn between irritation at him—how dare he be impatient at Mabel, it was hardly her fault she was in a space boot and she was doing extremely well considering she had a minor fracture in her ankle—and similar impatience. If Landon wasn't the one responsible, who was? Would Mat be at the Museum today? Would she be able to help them figure out who was behind the soft patches?

George caught himself speeding up and, like Landon, had to check his pace. He sighed and resolved to be more patient.

After all, Mabel *was* walking as fast as she could, and it wasn't like ten minutes was going to make that much of a difference really.

Still, he was extremely relieved when they entered the Museum and a warm blast of air welcomed them into the entry foyer. "Are you okay?" he said as he held the door open for Mabel; her face looked a little pale and drawn.

She nodded, but that in and of itself was a sign that she wasn't doing so well; she tended to go silent when she was really in pain.

"Come on, here," George said, shepherding her toward a low bench that had been moulded and painted to look like a banana split, the front slice of banana forming the actual seat. The room was much warmer than outside, and already George was beginning to sweat. He peeled off his outer jacket and laid it on the bench beside Mabel as she sat.

She still didn't say anything, but she leaned back on the bench and closed her eyes, easing her injured foot out in front of her.

Some of the tension left her shoulders.

"So," Landon said, looking around the foyer with an air of impatience, "where's this Mat woman you were talking about?"

"Do you mind if we go looking for a bit?" George said to Mabel.

She shook her head. "I'll be fine here. I know the desk person." She nodded toward the blue-and-cream information desk. The dark-haired woman working there nodded back.

George turned to Landon. "Right. Last time she was upstairs, in the Snow Queen exhibit."

Almost before George had finished talking, Landon was heading for the stairs, his bright red jacket a vibrant splash of colour against the caramel of the stair tiles and the gold of the waffle-textured balustrade. George sniffed and followed quickly, jumping up the first flight of stairs two at a time to catch up.

"This way," George said at the top, ducking in front of Landon and turning right.

He led Landon down the hallway to the Snow Queen exhibit, the large room with its glass-walled maze and pale blue lighting and the taste of ice in the air.

"Well?" said Landon, looking out of place with his bright red in the very blue room.

(But then, George supposed that he in his mustard-yellow jacket wasn't particularly more matching.)

"I don't know," George said. "This is where she was last time, but it's a big Museum! It's not like she has to stay in one exhibit or anything."

Landon opened his mouth—probably to argue—then stopped, pointing through the layers of glass walls with their photographs and plaques and displays that grew murkier and murkier the further away they were. "Someone's through there."

A shiver that was strong enough to be a shudder shook George as he spotted the person in the waffle-coloured pants and light blue shirt. "Might be her," he said, and stepped into the maze room.

At the first T-junction, George took the left turn.

"What are you doing?" Landon said. "We need to go this way!"

George glanced back down the right-hand walkway. It looked like it was heading closer toward the person who may or may not be Mat, but George was pretty sure that if they took that path, it twisted back the other way and ended up bypassing the spot they were trying to get to. He shook his head, squinting through the layers of the glass walls, trying to follow the paths in the dim blue light. "I don't think so," he said. "I think it's this way."

Landon shrugged. "Whatever. I'm going this way. Have fun wandering around lost for an hour." He strode down the walkway he'd picked, whistling tonelessly.

George rolled his eyes and continued left.

Sure enough, another two turns brought him right to the centre of the maze—and the woman who was indeed Mat turned to him and smiled.

A shiver rippled through him. Sure, the display was all about the Snow Queen, but did they have to have the air con working quite so ferociously? George tried to shrug the chill away.

"Hi," he said to Mat.

"Hello. What brings you here again so soon?"

George chewed on the inside of his lip. Where to start? Probably with the most important bit. He inhaled purposefully. "There was another soft patch. During the Junior semi-final. It tripped over... one of the other competitors."

A wrinkle creased Mat's brow momentarily. "Not you this time?"

"Well, I tripped over the other competitor," George said, "so kind of." His face heated; no worries now about the fierce air conditioning.

"Ah." Mat nodded, one decisive lifting of her chin. "Did you find the person you were looking for?"

"Sorry?"

"The person you were looking for. Last time you were here."

"Oh, him. Yeah, I—"

Landon's bright red jacket coalesced behind a pane of glass in the dim, blue light, like a whale shadow resolving in deep water. Or a shark.

A few more steps, and he joined them in the clear square at the middle of the maze, cheeks flushed.

George nodded. "That's him, actually," he said. "Mat, meet Landon, Landon, Mat."

Landon narrowed his eyes. "Don't I know you from somewhere?" he demanded.

Mat simply shrugged. "It's possible."

"Did you find out yet who's causing the soft patches?" Landon continued.

George didn't know which of them he was speaking to, but answered anyway. "No. I've only just got here."

"Well, we better *leave* here, and fast," Landon said, making as though to shoo them out the way George had come in—away from the hallway Landon had used. "Avi's back there and he's coming on like a freight train with a bee in its ear."

George blinked as he tried to sort through Landon's mixed metaphors, feeling a little as though the freight train had actually hit him. "Avi? What does *he* want?"

"Heck if I know," Landon said. "He's probably here to lodge some new complaint or other."

George frowned. Avi was always complaining about the races, about their safety, about... potholes.

George's heart skipped. He swung to Landon, eyes alight. "Landon, what if it's Avi?" he said. "You know about magic," he continued, pivoting to Mat. "Could you tell? Can you tell when you meet someone if they can do magic?"

Mat's gaze seemed to bore a hole right through him, and she held it just long enough that George felt his cheeks grow warm again; he dropped his gaze. But—

"Yes," she said simply.

George faced the maze's hallway eagerly, bouncing on his toes a little as Avi's shadow resolved in the dim light. The shush of the air conditioner filled George's awareness, both the sound of it and the way it brought the taste of ice to the back of his throat.

There, Avi was rounding the last corner...

"You!" he shouted as he spotted the trio of people waiting.

For a moment, George's pulse kicked as he thought Avi was pointing at him.

But Avi's gaze speared past George, straight to—Mat.

"It's all your fault!" Avi shouted—and leapt at the woman who was a member of the Museum's staff. "Always with this unnatural winter! Always with this cold! I want the *sun* back, and I want it back before the end of *spring*! Every year, the *cold*!"

Avi's shouts were so engrossing that it actually took George a second to realise what his eyes had already determined: Avi was trying hard to lash out at Mat, but something was holding him very firmly half an arm's length away.

George shivered.

Something...

Magic.

And around Mat, a gentle blue glow emanated, hard to see at first because it was the same colour as the lights in the maze—the Snow Queen's maze. The Snow Queen's maze where, twice now, he'd found this Museum woman called Mat.

George picked his mouth back up off the floor. "You're her," he said softly.

Her head swung round as though he'd tugged directly on her ear.

"The Snow Queen," George murmured.

A smile crashed over Mat's face and the glow around her intensified.

Avi was pushed back further, further, until he was stuck in the corner of the clear space, huddled up against the glass between a plaque that told the story of the Snow Queen's final battle with her nemesis in the Other World and a sepia photograph of, well, Mat.

"It is not he," Mat said quietly as Avi crumbled to the floor, hiding his face in his arms. "There is no magic in *his* soul."

Landon snorted. "No kidding," he said. "Wants the sun." He rolled his eyes. "What does he think happens every year in the summer? I swear, sometimes it gets so hot here I get burnt walking in the shade."

George shifted uncomfortably. Landon was right; Linderch was hardly Antarctic, or even boreal, with hot, steaming summers that still saw his father's melon vines curling over their trellis to bear fruit and the road shimmer with rising heat.

But Avi was right too. The winters *were* longer since the Snow Queen had arrived eight years ago. He was too young to remember it, but he'd seen the pictures his parents had from when he was little, when the warm weather lasted more than a few short, intense months.

And he could understand wanting things to stay the same, and resenting the ones who'd caused the changes.

He shook his head. "Yeah. It's not him."

But who *was* it, then?

His spine practically crawled, like the skin was trying to creep away, or like his bones were trying to get out.

Come on, George. Think!

Someone who wants the races cancelled.

Someone who wants me and Mabel out of the race?

His breath caught.

No. It couldn't be.

George ran through it all again, checking and double checking. He might be wrong… But the evidence fit—and, more than that, the crawling of his spine told him he was probably—definitely—right.

He looked up—and Mat was staring right at him, a knowing expression slightly crinkling her eyes. George smiled grimly back. "I've got it," he said. "I know who's responsible for the soft patches."

Landon jerked in surprise, but Mat simply nodded. "Yes," she said. "I rather think you do."

CHAPTER 9

AS THEY STRODE BACK INTO THE CROWD AT THE ICE CREAM pond, George leading the way and Mabel bringing up the rear with her hobbling gait, people parted left and right like a tide. Any other time, George might have enjoyed it. But right now, with the cold air slapping life into his cheeks and invigorating his lungs, he was so full of energy he thought he might burst.

Somewhere here, in this crowd, was the person responsible for the soft patches in the ice cream. George could sense it.

"This way," he said, glancing back at Mat—and doing a double take as he realised an ephemeral silvery crown had appeared over her head, made entirely out of light.

No wonder people were backing away and staring.

George grinned fiercely.

He led the small group past an ice cream stall, its waffle-cone machines running at full speed and filling the air with their warm, sugary smell. He wound along the path that led to the main viewing area, the chatter of the group dimming to hushed whispers as they recognised the Snow Queen.

And finally, he stopped at the foot of the white wooden bleachers, staring up at the rows of faces, most of whom stared back.

"There," he said. A rippling shudder of satisfaction went through him. Right there.

But beside him, the Snow Queen frowned. "Are you sure?"

George's eyebrows climbed. "Can't *you* tell?" he asked.

On the other side, Landon muttered something inaudible.

Mat pursed her lips. "No. But I trust your judgement. Which one is it?"

George's stomach fluttered. The Snow Queen trusted *him*? But... what if he'd gotten it wrong?

He ran his gaze over the rows of faces again.

One in particular stared back with eyes narrowed and mouth twisted in disgust.

"Snow Queen? What's going on here?"

It was Audrey, one white boot only half zipped over her silver tights, her silver tutu catching the light and throwing it back glitteringly—and still nowhere near as bright as the silver crown of light over the Snow Queen's head.

"Someone has been cheating," Mat said, only giving Audrey a cursory glance.

"Cheating?!" Audrey's eyes went saucer-wide.

"Someone has been using magic to tamper with the pond."

Still wide-eyed, Audrey turned to George. "Is this... Is this about the soft patches you were talking about?"

George bit back a vicious grin. "Yes." Vindication was sweet as sugary waffle cones.

A movement on the bleachers caught his eye.

Max.

Max-From-The-Bank, Max the Saboteur, Max the one who, for whatever reason, wanted George and Mabel out of the races so badly that he was willing to reveal his magic to make it happen.

"Stop him!" George shouted as Max got to the end of the top row of the bleachers and started down the stairs.

Confusion reigned, half the spectators staring open mouthed at George, half looking wildly around for whatever it was George was pointing at—and the rest just ignoring the shenanigans entirely.

Max grabbed the handrails and vaulted clean over the edge of the bleachers, disappearing almost as soon as he landed in the slushy snow behind them.

George sprinted to head him off.

But there was no need. The crown gasped—and over George's head, a lance of ice-cold light flew, right at Max's rapidly retreating back.

George stumbled to a halt as the ice lance hit Max and dropped him to the ground. Clutching his side where a stitch had grabbed, George stared down at Max in disbelief.

Ordinarily, Max-From-The-Bank was a medium height man with light brown curls and fair skin. But now...

The Snow Queen arrived, stopping at George's shoulder. Mabel and Landon hurried up on the other side.

"Yes," the Snow Queen said. "I see him now."

"Me too," said George fervently, kind of wishing he couldn't. Because now, Max's skin had taken on a glistening blue sheen, and through his hair stuck two pointed horns, curved like a bull but crystalline—like they were made from ice. The effect wasn't *monstrous*, the calm and rational part of George's mind decided, but it was definitely both unexpected and unsettling.

Max squirmed on the ground, pinned by whatever magic the Snow Queen had used to unmask him.

In fact...

George tilted his head.

Something between his shoulder blades itched; if he turned his head just right, it was almost like he could see something, a strange iridescence of some kind, almost like a barely visible cage pinning Max to the slushy snow beneath him.

Max glared up at them, seething. "You've ruined

everything," he spat at George—then actually spat at him. The Snow Queen's cage kept it in, but Max barely even seemed to notice that his saliva had fallen back on his face. "You couldn't just fall neatly now, could you," he continued. "Had to go and get *her* involved, had to weasel me out… All I wanted was to go home."

George's eyes had grown wider. "You know…" He glanced up at the Snow Queen beside him—had she gotten taller since they'd left the Museum?—then back at Max. "Mat?"

"Yes," Max snarled, hands curled into fists at his sides. "I know *Mat*. I know your precious *Snow Queen*, and all she does, and all she's done, and all she'll ever be."

George frowned, turning to the Snow Queen. "He knows you? But you didn't recognise him. What does he mean?"

The Snow Queen sighed heavily, gaze never leaving Max. "You've read my story in the Museum, haven't you? Why did I come here?"

"Because you retired," he said, his frown deepening in thought. "After bringing peace to your realm."

The Snow Queen tsked. "Yes, yes, and how did I *do* that?"

"You beat your nem… e… sis…" The word dribbled out of George's mouth in pieces as his brain raced instead. "*Max* is your *nemesis*?"

"In disguise, apparently, but yes." The Snow Queen nodded.

"What do you mean, you want to go home?" Mabel said softly—and George jumped a little. His world had narrowed almost entirely to the two magical beings—Two of them! Two! Within arm's reach!—and he'd forgotten he wasn't the only one with a stake in this particular race.

Abruptly, the sneer on Max's face crumbled, and he stilled. "Your house," he said, and he sounded tired. "It's the only place to cross safely between the dimensions, unless you have enough power to cross by yourself."

George frowned. Everyone knew the legend: the Snow Queen had fought for peace and stability in her realm, and then, when she'd finally defeated her nemesis and appointed a wise and sensible successor, had cross into the Earthly Realm to retire.

Nothing in the story hinted at anything else having the ability to cross between Earth and the Other World—but then again, wasn't what Max said about George's family house right?

Wasn't that the whole point, the whole reason the family had tried so hard to stay there—because there was something magical, something Other Worldly about it?

George shook his head. "But you're her nemesis, the Snow Queen's great rival. Surely you have enough power to cross between the magical world and the physical one as well, don't you?"

The Snow Queen shifted at his side, and when George glanced up, her eyes were sad and thoughtful. “Only two people ever had the power to do that,” she said, quiet, wistful.

“Yes,” Max agreed sourly. “And you did everything within your power to make sure that that number was reduced by half.”

“I wouldn’t have had to,” said the Snow Queen, arching an eyebrow, “if you hadn’t threatened to destroy the physical plane if you didn’t get your own way in the magical one.”

George blinked. “He did what?”

Around them, George could sense the interest of the crowd like something tangible, a thread of attention wrapping tightly around them all, like the taste of waffle cones in the back of your throat, or the smell of snow on heavy laden clouds, background noise until you focused on it and realised just how sharp a thing it was.

People shuffled a little nearer, not wanting to miss a word.

The Snow Queen waggled her head, one eye squinting in thought, even though her gaze still didn’t leave Max. “He could have been king,” she said. “Instead of me being queen. But centuries ago, there was a vote, and they picked me. He never forgave me for that.”

“I would have done a much better job,” Max said sulkily.

The Snow Queen snorted. “You let the trolls take over the magic mirror because they promised they’d bring you back gold. They double-crossed you, stole the mirror, and threw the entire realm into a sixty-year season of *slaughter*. And you wanted everyone to vote for you after *that*?"

A cold wind gusted up off the pond, over the transfixed crowd. Somewhere in the thick crush of people, a toddler cried out, only to be hurriedly hushed.

The smell of burnt sugar curled in the wake of the gusty wind.

"So what happened?" George glanced back and forth between the two magical beings, hungry in a way he couldn't quite articulate, in the pit of his stomach, to know the rest of the story.

"I banished him," the Snow Queen said simply, and all of a sudden she was no longer the Snow Queen, but was once more Mat, the ordinary-looking woman George had met in the Museum. That, and she looked tired around the eyes. "I banished him, only he convinced the trolls to bring him here as compensation for double-crossing him nearly a century ago, but now he can't get back again. Doesn't have the power to go himself, and no one else wants to come get him." She smiled, sadly and not unkindly.

Max's smile, on the other hand, was all tooth, and George felt instantly on alert, shivers sliding up and down his spine. "I haven't been doing nothing this whole time," Max said, and it was the quiet voice of a predator's footsteps in the jungle.

George found himself inching away, and forced his feet to stop.

"I've learned a few things."

One second, Max was lying on the ground, safe in the Snow Queen's barely visible cage.

The next, he lunged at the Mat, outstretched hands looking suddenly like they ended in claws. A scream of rage issued from him.

Lightning cracked.

Around them, the clouds flooded open and snow billowed down, forming a ring around the pond.

Lightning came again, this time arching from Max's fingers toward Mat, toward the Snow Queen—

And George, entirely on instinct, flung himself in the path of the lightning, in the way of the Snow Queen—and stretched out his hand.

The lightning hit it.

George took it in.

It poured into him, filling him to the brim, hot, burning, searing...

And he flung it out through his other hand, down deep into the ground.

The earth shook.

Snow melted where George fell as he landed.

As abruptly as it had all started, the lightning and snowfall were gone.

The clouds rolled away as though engine-powered, and in an instant bright sunlight flooded the scene.

People winced and shielded their eyes, George among them.

Then, slowly, hesitantly at first, applause broke out. Cheers joined the clapping, and the noise built to a crescendo: the whole crowd, cheering and clapping and some even crying, because there was Max, trapped—only this time, the cage was entirely visible, and it was a little patchy, thick in some places and thin in others, like someone who didn't really know what they were doing had made it.

"Let me take that from you," Mat said quietly as she stooped to the ground where George was lying, breathing heavily, sweat dripping down one temple.

"What?" George said thickly.

"That." She tilted her head toward Max, toward his haphazardly constructed prison.

"Oh." That. George flexed his hand—and the cage rippled in response. "Oh." Adrenalin pumped through him, his stomach doing something complicated—and he was exhausted. "Oh, uh, yeah." He glanced at Mat. "How do I do that, exactly?" He could sense, now, where the magic was connected to him—but he had no idea how to let it go.

"Here," Mat said, and reached out, and took it from him. "You did very well," she said, patting his shoulder before standing.

The rippling light around Max faded back to virtual invisibility almost at once.

Mabel darted forward, as nimbly as she could, and helped George to his feet. To his surprise, Landon was there on the other side, lifting him just as supportively at Mabel.

"Nice work," Landon said, a little grudgingly, just as he would acknowledge a really good move out on the ice by a competitor he respected.

"Nice!" Mabel's voice was practically shrill with outrage. "Nice! That was *incredible*, George! Where did you learn to do that?"

George shook his head. He opened his mouth, but somehow he'd forgotten how to make the words come out.

And then his parents were there, breathing hard like they'd run all the way from where they'd been watching the races on the other side of the pond, and his mum and dad were holding him close and Mat was reassuring him that he was fine, he just needed to sit down for a minute and get some fluids.

George was sat firmly on the lowest level of the bleachers, and a bottle full of blue fake-berry sports drink was pushed into his hand.

"I guess this means I should let you race in the finals," a voice said in George's ear as the crowd's murmuring began to resume something like normal levels, and the knot of interest around him was drifting away.

He glanced up, startled, to find Audrey leaning close, a grin on her face.

The cold of the sports drink hit George's stomach like a shot of pure energy. George grinned. "I'd guess you'd better," he said.

The finals. The finals! He was going to get a shot

at the finals after all. Which, Max might be gone—but the bank still needed the last few months' mortgage payments, or George and his family would lose the house regardless.

He screwed up his face. "Not sure I'll be ready to race in the next half hour, though."

Audrey nodded at the crowd; a few younger children had broken away from their parents and were daring to approach the Snow Queen, timid until she gave them an encouraging nod, and then faster, with grins as bright as the sunshine above. "I have a feeling the finals won't be running on time." Her eyes sparkled. "I'll give you, what, an hour? Two?" She nodded, agreeing with her own suggestion. "I'll give you two hours," she said. "No one will mind hanging out for a wee bit longer, given all the excitement." She winked. "See you at the starting line." And she slipped away back into the crowd, weaving her way toward the competitors' marshalling area.

George blinked as he watched her go.

The finals.

He was going to be in the finals after all.

And Max had been dealt with.

Maybe they really would get to keep their house after all.

CHAPTER 10

GEORGE RACED ACROSS THE FINISH LINE, SKATES SHISHING on the ice, with only a couple of paces between him and Landon.

His heart nearly burst—and not just from the exertion.

Vaguely, he could hear the crowd going wild as he, the late-comer and significant underdog, won the Junior Finals. Hardly anyone had expected that he would, but people did love a long shot.

Mostly, though, he could hear the sound of his own heartbeat, thundering in his ears; could taste the sweat at the corners of his mouth now that his focus was off the race; could feel the way the cold air sucked into his chest, filling him right, right up, like he was a balloon that might fly away with each breath.

Like relief.

Like he'd won.

Landon swerved to a stop right in front of him.

For a moment, George's stomach flipped. Landon had been pretty supportive of George since the whole Max event, but even so, it wasn't exactly like they were *friends*, and George *had* just beaten him...

But Landon gave a decisive nod. "Nice skating," he said. Then he spun and skated away again, calling over his shoulder, "I nearly had you on the Mint Choc Dip. Don't expect to beat me again."

George laughed. Was he imagining things, or was the sun really brighter than it had been this morning? He skated back to the competitors' marshalling area, where the snow on the shore glittered and sparkled. Mabel hobbled to meet him, throwing her arms around him and squeezing him tight. "Hey," George said, wincing. "I need to breathe!"

She pushed him away, laughing, tears running down her face.

"Hey," George said, catching her by the wrist and pulling her back again. He swiped at the tears on her cheek. "I won. It's all going to be okay."

She nodded, eyes shining bright. "I know. I know. You did it." She laughed again, then sniffed and wiped her face herself. "Come on," she said, tugging at his arm. "Mum and Dad will want to congratulate you."

George paused long enough to take his skates off and replace them with his warm boots, then followed Mabel up the slope to where Mum and

Dad pressed against the fence, grinning like they might burst.

Mum squeezed him even tighter than Mabel had over the sheep panel fence, the top rail a rod of ice between them that didn't detract even in the slightest from the warmth of excitement. Dad gave him a hug too, then patted him on the head, ruffling up his knitted beanie and consequently his hair underneath. "Well done, kiddo," he said.

"You know what the prize is though, right?" George said quietly—or as quietly as he could and still be heard over the crowd, buzzing from the results of the Junior Finals and simultaneously getting hyped up, ready for the Open Finals.

Confusion flickered over Dad's face for a second. "What do you mean?"

"Eight thousand dollars to first place," Mabel piped up, grinning.

"I'm giving it to you guys," George said. "It's for the house payments."

Mum's mouth fell open into an O. Dad blinked.

"We also get a lifetime supply of ice cream."

George's grin was even wider than Mabel's at that, especially since it had the effect of deepening their parents' confusion instead of resolving it.

"A lifetime supply of ice cream?" Mum said, eyebrows rising. "But... what on *earth* are we going to do with that? Your father and I are lactose intolerant!"

George and Mabel grinned at each other. "Well, first of all, I'm pretty sure the Snow Queen does sorbet as well," George said. "But secondly, we're not planning to *keep* it."

The crowd ebbed and flowed around them, scents shifting from waffle cone to something sharply acidic; lemon, maybe, or possibly lime, it was hard to tell.

George inhaled deeply with satisfaction. Yes, it was a good thing he appreciated the smell of ice cream, because—

Mabel practically bounced, despite her space boot. "We're going to *sell* it," she said, unable to withhold the punchline any longer.

"A lifetime supply of ice cream"—George held one hand out as though weighing something in it—"a lifetime supply of a popular product to profit from." He raised his other hand, then shifted both hands up and down until the two came into balance. "We can run a family business that will actually be successful, and Dad can finish his studying."

Dad reeled back a little, gripping the top rail of the fence and leaning back until his arms were at full stretch.

Mum blinked. Once, then rapidly, then even more rapidly as her eyes welled.

They glanced at each other. "But we can't—" Dad said at the same time as Mum said, "Is it *legal*?"

George shrugged. "There's nothing in the rules that says we have to keep the ice cream to ourselves, or that we can't on-sell it," he said. "We checked."

"Twice," Mabel added.

Mum's welling eyes became flooding eyes, and Dad began to look distinctly misty-eyed as well. He swallowed hard. "Son. Mabel." His gaze took them both in, fairly busting with pride—and relief.

It was the least stressed George remembered seeing his father in... maybe years, honestly.

As if by mutual agreement, the four of them leaned in together.

"Family hug!" Mabel shouted, her line by right of being the youngest.

The others laughed.

Someone tapped George on the shoulder.

He jerked around.

"Sorry to interrupt the moment," Audrey said. "But you're needed." She nodded back to the marshalling area, where the Snow Queen stood waiting by the podium, lit up in her full glory, glowing silver with her silver-and-ice crown gleaming in the light.

The Snow Queen waved calmly.

"I'll be back," George told his family. "And then we can all go home together."

CHAPTER 11

THE HOUSE STILL HAD MOMENTS WHERE RANDOM SMELLS drifted through the hallways, unpleasant and often unfamiliar. George and Mabel had decided, after long conversations with Mat—she insisted that they call her that now, no 'Snow Queen' allowed—that it was simply a consequence of the house drifting across the dimensions. Sometimes it was the view out the window that changed, and sometimes it was a stray smell. What could you do, when you chose to live in an interdimensional portal like that?

Mostly, however, the house smelled of waffle cones. Mum had discovered, during some late night research, that due to some old zoning laws that everyone *thought* had been rewritten but that, due to a tiny loophole, could still be enforced, it was actually legal for them to run a shopfront right there from their house.

And so that's what they did. Being across the opposite side of town as they were to the Museum, they had a steady enough trickle of customers that Dad didn't have to try to find more work; and Mat herself came by often enough, sometimes with a tub of a special, limited-edition ice cream flavour (the lemon meringue twirl had been George's favourite, though Mabel had preferred the double-choc-chunk cheesecake ice cream, and neither of them had been particularly fans of the highly experimental mushroom ice cream, though the green pea and mint had been surprisingly not bad and had proved somewhat popular with people in their thirties—who could have known?) and sometimes just to hang out in the little parlour room at the front of the house with its squishy couches and a wall full of board games and the two big bains marie full of different ice cream tubs.

Mabel had learned to curl the perfect scoop, and took immense pride in showing off her ability.

Privately, George was just happy to know he wasn't going to have to move, that this small, squishy, smelly old house was theirs, now and probably forever, and that, even if he *did* occasionally spot something that looked suspiciously like a troll as the evening light stole across the small concrete square of the backyard, no one else was going to try to take it from them.

Besides. Sitting at the kitchen table, staring out at the yard over the sink, he grinned. Both his hands were resting on the table in front of him, palms up... and over his left hand, a tiny, perfect snowflake was spinning.

If anyone else tried to take their house from them again, well, this time, George would have a surprise for them, because it wasn't only people who'd been born in the magical plane who could learn to use magic.

And George, under Mat's excellent tutelage, was a very fast learner.

ABOUT THE AUTHOR

AMY LAURENS is an award-winning Australian fantasy author. She has written the *Sanctuary* trilogy for upper middle grade readers (a portal fantasy set in Australia, with unicorns, fairies of ambiguous morality, and soul-sucking shadows), the *Kaditeos* series of comic fantasy stories, mostly centring around the newly graduated Evil Overlord Mercury and her attempts to take control of her kingdom, and the *Storm Foxes* series about love and mental health in small-town Australia—with magical stormy foxes.

Amy has also written a host of non-fiction, some for writers (including the popular *How To Theme* and *How To Create Cultures*) and some for people who *don't* spend their entire lives glued to the keyboard typing out the instructions given by the voices in their head (*The 32 Worst Mistakes People Make About Dogs, How To Plan A Pinterest-Worthy Party Without Dying*).

You can find out more about Amy at her website, www.AmyLaurens.com.

Also by Amy Laurens:

WHERE SHADOWS RISE
Sanctuary #1

All is not well in fairy land...

WHERE SHADOWS RISE
CHAPTER ONE

THE DOORBELL RANG. That doesn't sound exciting in and of itself, but let me assure you: it was the most heart-pounding thing to happen all week. It was my birthday, I was home alone, and because of the stupid witness protection business, I'd been stuck in the house all summer. I hadn't even been allowed out to see friends, because we'd arrived in town at the end of last year with only three school weeks to go—so I didn't have any friends.

Well. I had friends, but they were back in Melbourne, and I wasn't allowed to contact them for fear someone would track down our new location. Lucky me.

Anyway, it was my birthday, I was alone because Mum and Dad had gone to do something regarding birthday surprises and Anna had inexplicably chosen to go with them, and the doorbell had just rung. I stared at the closed door, heart pounding, while our chocolate Labrador,

Veve, tried to chew it down. Was I going to open it?

Of course I was going to open it. The chances of it being a mobster were slim to none; for starters, a mobster wouldn't have rung the bell.

I opened it.

"Miss Tanning?" The deliveryman raised a questioning eyebrow and cocked a digital pen at me.

I nodded, heart flip-flopping, and scrawled a fair impersonation of my signature on the digital pad.

He handed over a small, brown-paper parcel with a handwritten address, and departed.

I closed the door behind him, throat dry, and stared down at Veve. On the one hand, yay birthday present. On the other, holy crap, someone had our address. That was *not* a good thing.

It became even less of a good thing when I noticed that the parcel was indeed addressed to a Miss Tanning: a Miss *Anna* Tanning, as in my sister, not me, Emma Tanning.

Anger bubbled up in my chest, hot and tight, and the parcel protested in my grip.

Veve whined softly.

"How could she *do* this?" I whispered to Veve.

I turned the parcel over. It was from Kade, Anna's frogging ex-boyfriend. Who apparently wasn't an 'ex' after all.

Urgh. I ground my teeth. "You know what?" I asked Veve.

She looked up at me with her liquid brown eyes, tongue lolling as she smiled.

"Screw it. If Anna can get interstate mail from

people who aren't even supposed to know we exist anymore, you and I can go for a walk on my birthday. What do you think?"

They say dogs don't speak English, but Veve sure as heck knew the word 'walk'—though I think in her vocabulary it was something closer to 'Magical Trip To Disneyland' and less like 'Comparatively Bland Meander Through Trees'. She tucked her tail right under her butt and shot down the hall, whirling in frantic circles a few times at the end before pelting back as I retrieved her lead from the drawer in the front cabinet.

I rolled my eyes as I clipped her lead onto her collar. For my troubles, I got slimed right up the nostrils. "You're disgusting, you know that?" I wiped off the worst of the dog slobber on the shoulder of my shirt. She just grinned.

Out on the street, she leapt and twisted madly. "Hair-brain," I told her, snapping the lead to get her attention. "It's just a walk."

She just snorted—and stiffened. I followed her gaze to where a flock of corellas pecked their way through the dry grass at the end of the street.

"Veve!"

My shout was in vain: the lead burned through my fingers and Veve shot down the road, a chocolate bullet howling death and destruction for all things feathered.

I cursed her to the lower circles of doggie hell. Which probably involved, I don't know, a world devoid of birds, cats, people, sunshine, and walks, if Veve was anything to go by.

"Veve!" If the sight of the mad Lab-rat barrelling toward them hadn't scared the birds off, my shouts would have. "Come back here *now*!"

Predictably, she ignored me, pounding down the slope, through the fringe of gum trees, and down the narrow stairs between giant granite boulders that led to the river.

"Stupid frogging brainless beast of a stupid frogging dog," I muttered as I followed. "If Mum gets home before we do and freaks out, I swear, I'll pluck your tail hairs out."

Empty threats, obviously, but Mum's freak-out wouldn't be. Her thoughts would go straight to the day Anna nearly died—and I wouldn't blame her. I should have left a note. Urgh.

The stairs ended and I found myself on a track broad enough for two twisting along a creek the colour of bitter tea. Tussock grass clustered in spikes—where the eucalypts would let it—and hot summer sunlight glinted from the leaves. Somewhere to my right, downstream and in the opposite direction to the house, Veve barked. I exhaled like a whale coming up for air and set out after her.

Veve bounded out from the undergrowth in front of me, a dolphin leaping through water, tongue flapping with every bound. "Stupid mutt," I told her under my breath.

She didn't care what I thought (of course), and saved a leap for the last minute so she could plant muddy feet on my hips as I tried to catch her collar.

I straightened, about to insult her some more, and realised that she'd gone stiff again, ears pricked and mouth tight, listening down the path.

My neck prickled. Someone was coming. A second later, I heard footsteps in the gravel, and a low, male voice, humming, or maybe singing softly.

My chest constricted, and just as suddenly my hands were slick. Chances were it was just a stranger out for a midday stroll, but my stomach wound knots about my memories and I smelled the hot concrete and melting asphalt, old oil and stale urine of the Lilydale train station where the body had been hidden in a toilet stall, the body of the girl who'd looked like Anna.

I had to get off the path.

"Come on, Veve," I said, pulling her close, white-knuckled as I stepped into the undergrowth. The tea tree scrub protested, but I shoved my way through anyway, glancing over my shoulder as the humming grew louder.

I kept going until I couldn't hear footsteps any more, until the wind swallowed the hum that sounded too like the warning cry of a hive—danger, we're working here, come close and get stung.

I didn't want to get stung; visions of a blood-streaked face refused to be blinked away. Only Veve tugging brought me back to myself, and I realised firstly that I was holding the lead way too tight, cutting off Veve's air supply, secondly that the reason my cheeks were suddenly cold was because I'd been crying, and thirdly that I'd found the creek again, looping back parallel maybe fifty meters or so from the path.

Abruptly, I dropped Veve's lead and strode forward to kneel by the water. I dipped my hands in. A shiver slide through me at its chill, and I scooped it up to wash my face.

Flinging the excess water away, I gulped at the air, deep, calming breaths all the way down into my belly, and visualised a river washing away the blood from my thoughts, just like the police psych had taught me.

Once the space behind my eyes was calm and black, I drew in one last forceful breath, and opened my eyes. Perched on a rock by the creek, I hugged my knees to my chest as cool water lapped at my toes. Veve was a little upstream, just before the creek bent back toward the path, doggy paddling in circles in a deep spot where the water broadened to maybe ten meters across. In front of me it was broad but shallow, only ankle deep, its path torn to white foam by the rocks.

And—I gasped. In the middle of the stream, glittering in the sun like a piece of fallen sky, was the hugest butterfly I'd ever seen. Which was pretty huge; besides the fact that I grew up visiting the Melbourne Zoo with its impressive butterfly house every Christmas since I could remember, Mum and Dad had taken us up to Brisbane for a family holiday two years ago, and we'd seen giant tropical butterflies bigger than my hand.

This one, bright blue with black edging like a Ulysses, was bigger than both my hands put together.

And then it turned around.

Okay. I'd grown up reading fairy tales as much as the next person, and although I'd had a horse-crazy stage instead of a fairy-crazy stage like Anna had, I'd seen all her paraphernalia. Still, none of it prepared me for finding something that looked exactly like a fairy, standing smack in the middle of a creek in boring, backwater Nowra. I'm pretty sure my eyes were only hanging in their sockets by a thread.

And then it talked.

Her face lit up like a cloud had just uncovered the sun as she spotted me. "Hi there!" she said, fluttering over.

I just stared, heart pounding against my ribcage as though it wanted to run away from the absurdity of it all. "No," I said. "I'm hallucinating."

The fairy frowned. "I don't think so."

I shook my head. "No. No, things like this do not happen. Things like this aren't *real*." I stood, backing up a step.

The fairy sighed. "I promise. I'm quite real."

"You would say that, wouldn't you," I said, eyeing her. "Veve!" I waved at the dog and hopped from one foot to the other, trying to lure her in with the promise of play. "We're going now!"

Veve, adorable beast that she was, landed a little upstream and shook vigorously before trotting toward me. I backed hurriedly away from the bank, dancing to keep Veve's attention.

"Wait!" the fairy cried, wings snapping out and propelling her a couple of feet into the air. "You're a Traveller! I need to talk to you!"

"Uh huh, sure," I said as I wound the lead around my hand and set off back into the bushes. This was punishment for leaving the house, obviously. The universe was out to get me, reminding me forcefully that once you started disregarding some rules, who knew what other rules you'd end up flouting.

The rules of physics, for example.

I glanced back once, right before the bushes hid the stream altogether. Blue flashed, high up, but I ducked to get a better view and it was only the sky. I scowled. Stupid fairy. Stupid universe. Served me right for leaving the house in the first place. Urgh. "Come on, Veve," I said, snapping the lead. "Even if the house is prison, at least it's *sane*."

I was stomping so furiously as I burst out onto the path that when a figure rose from a stoop only a couple of steps away, I squeaked in surprise.

I scowled. People rarely surprised me; usually I could tell without trying that someone was near. I really must have been off in my own little world.

I glowered at the boy who lived to make my school life a misery. "What are you doing here?" I snapped. "Isn't it bad enough that I have to deal with you on school days? Which, by the way, don't start until tomorrow. You're ruining my holidays."

Okay, so maybe that was a little harsh, but come on. It was *Scott*. I'd arrived in town with three weeks left in the school year, and he'd spent every day of them humiliating me in front of his mates, and I didn't care for a repeat this year.

Scott eyed me warily, which was a strange expression on him. Usually he strode around like he knew without a doubt that he was too good for the world, and also—somewhere deeper, somewhere I'd only caught a glimpse of once or twice—that it had nothing left to throw at him that could hurt.

Occasionally, in my more generous moments, I wondered what had happened to make him look that way. Mostly, however, I just wondered why he was such a moron.

"What are you doing here?" he asked, voice dripping with accusation and suspicion.

My hands fisted of their own accord, and beside me Veve's hackles rose as she chimed in with a low-pitched, rumbling growl. I flicked the free end of the lead at her nose. "Nothing," I said, in a rousing blaze of wit. "What are you doing?"

He scowled. "You shouldn't be here."

For one heart-stopping instant I thought he meant out here generally, walking around, as if he knew what had happened and why I'd hidden away all summer. Then I realised he was nodding into the undergrowth. I rolled my eyes. "I might be a city slicker," I bit off, "but I'm not stupid. I made enough noise to scare off a herd of elephants, let alone any snakes that might have been lying around." The thought chilled me, though; I *hadn't* been thinking about snakes when I'd hurried off the path. One badly-timed footstep and a brown snake bite later, and I could be a dead body too.

But Scott had moved on, stalking off down the path. He had nice shoulders, I'd give him that much. Pity he couldn't derive his personality from them, instead of whatever dead weight it was he kept inside his head for brains.

Beside me, Veve growled again, louder this time, more urgent. I snapped the lead at her and stared after Scott's retreating form, trying to think of something cutting.

It was only when Veve growled for the third time that I realised she wasn't even facing Scott. Instead, she was looking back into the bushes—and something dark was flickering in there, deep in the shadows of the trees.

My chest squeezed in on itself and adrenalin shot through my body. Veve's growling grew louder until it broke in a bark, something midway between slavering and terrified, and I realised my tongue was stuck to the roof of my mouth. Carefully I peeled it away, unable to tear my eyes from the shifting darkness in the bushes. There was no discernible form, just shadow, darker than it should have been this soon after midday, and a pervasive sense of dread clamping down on me like an on-coming storm.

Veve began backing away, hackles prickling,

growl rising and falling like thunder. I glanced down at her, back to the shadows—and they were closer, much closer than they had been.

I turned and bolted.

Keep reading!
www.inkprintpress.com/ amylaurens/sanctuary/shadows/

Milton Keynes UK
Ingram Content Group UK Ltd.
UKHW011817120624
444110UK00004B/132